W9-BVT-466

LA 2011
C-10

CHICAGO PUBLIC LIBRARY

HAROLD A BEZAZIAN BRANCH
1226 W. AINSLIE STREET
CHICAGO, ILLINOIS 60640

FORM 19

IDUNA

AND THE MAGIC APPLES

by Marianna Mayer

illustrated by Laszlo Gal

Macmillan Publishing Company   New York

Collier Macmillan Publishers   London

FOR GERALD—M.M.

FOR PINTÉR FERENC—L.G.

Text copyright © 1988 by Marianna Mayer • Illustrations copyright © 1988 by Laszlo Gal

All rights reserved. No part of this book may be reproduced or transmitted in any form or by any means, electronic or mechanical, including photocopying, recording, or by any information storage and retrieval system, without permission in writing from the Publisher.
Macmillan Publishing Company, 866 Third Avenue, New York, NY 10022. Collier Macmillan Canada, Inc. Printed and bound in Japan. First American Edition   10   9   8   7   6   5   4   3   2   1

The text of this book is set in 14 point Cochin. The illustrations are rendered in a resin-color wash with egg tempera on paper.

LIBRARY OF CONGRESS CATALOGING-IN-PUBLICATION DATA   Mayer, Marianna. Iduna and the magic apples. Summary: The evil giant Thiassi vows to capture Iduna and her magic apples which give the gods on Valhalla everlasting life. 1. Idun (Norse deity) – Juvenile literature. [1. Idun (Norse deity) 2. Mythology, Norse] I. Gál, László, ill. II. Title. BL870.I38M39   1988   293′.13   88-2494   ISBN 0-02-765120-7

THE CHICAGO PUBLIC LIBRARY
Bezazian Branch
1226 W. Ainslie
Chicago, IL 60640

AUTHOR'S NOTE

The Norse myth of Iduna and the magic apples can be found in two early sources: the tenth-century poem *Haustlong* composed by Thildolf of Hvin, a poet of southern Norway; and the thirteenth-century *Prose Edda* recorded by the Icelandic scholar Snorri Sturluson.

Iduna belongs to the Aesir, that race of Nordic gods and goddesses who inhabit the land of Asgard. Translated, Iduna means "renewal" or "the renewing one." Her image is eternal youth. As the keeper of the golden apples, she holds the gift of immortality. It is she who ensures that the gods remain eternally young. Without her the season turns forever to the dead of winter, the flowers wither, and the gods begin to age.

Like all myths regardless of their origin, Iduna's haunting tale was born out of a need to explain the inexplicable. From pagan times to the present, we have used myths, *the first stories*, to help us understand ourselves, our origins, and creation itself. For these reasons, Iduna's tale, in all its timeless beauty, has been preserved throughout the centuries.

In an ancient time, when the Norse gods dwelt in the land called Asgard, the wind blew through the halls of their splendid palaces and listened to their tales. The wind was young as a summer breeze, blowing from wild, wooded gardens to lush green valleys where only the gods walked. Although such times are past, the wind remembers the stories of the gods. If you listen carefully, you may hear it whisper the tale of Iduna and the magic apples... how her treasure of golden apples kept the great god Odin, his brother Loki, and all the other gods from growing old... but the wicked giant Thiassi envied the gods and sought to bring ruin upon them...

once upon a time....

Of all the gardens in Asgard, none was more beautiful than Iduna's. The great lord Odin and the other gods named it Everlasting, for from the moment Iduna entered it, nothing withered, nothing died. Flowers blue and lavender, crimson and yellow, palest pink and fairest white, grew in glorious abundance, rivaling each other in radiance. Trees bore throughout the year—brilliant blossoms and sweet fruit together upon the same bough. The grass was fair and tender green, as in the first few days of spring, and in Iduna's garden it was *always* spring.

The wind's gentle breezes blew through the grove and whispered softly to the fresh young flowers. *Dance as I blow. Toss your pretty heads this way and that. You'll never tire. You'll never fade. Iduna looks after you.* Hearing the wind's song, the birds took up the chant and sang it as they flew throughout the garden.

In this splendid garden, Iduna was a fitting mistress. Her sweet temper and natural beauty drew the wild swans to rest their heads upon her lap. The birds always sang their best songs for her. Indeed, all the wild beasts loved her. Even the fish in the lake grew tame at the sight of her strolling by the water and came swimming to the surface to gaze at her with love.

In all the time she had lived in the garden, Iduna had never left it. It was her sanctuary. So long as she remained within its walls, no harm could come to her or those she loved. But should she leave...what then? Many things would change.

This little paradise was a happy place. Odin and the other gods often visited, marveling at Iduna's kindness and delighting in her humor and her wit. Yet there was another reason that they came: Iduna possessed a special treasure — a golden chest of magic apples that kept all those who ate them ever young. Truly it was the precious fruit that kept the gods immortal. Odin knew the value of these apples. He never ventured on a journey without a few to take along.

This very day he had come with his half brother Loki to see Iduna. They were setting off on foot to tour the ordinary world disguised as peasants, wishing to observe it unrecognized. Iduna made them a gift of all the magic apples she had. But no sooner had she emptied the chest than it refilled itself.

It was late afternoon when Iduna said farewell to her friends and walked down to the riverbank. There she sat, watching the sky reflected on the slowly moving water. Dreamily she looked on as the mirrored faces of the clouds changed from rose to crimson in the setting sun.

All at once, a startling shadow fell across the water. It was huge and dark with widespread wings. Iduna looked up and gasped in horror. A monstrous figure — a bird with a menacing human face — glowered at her. She tried to look away, she tried to run, but the creature's piercing gaze was too compelling. She could not move.

Then abruptly the monster drew itself up and, curling its sharp talons, flew higher and higher into the sky. The power of Iduna's garden had protected her. The monster wished to capture her, but he would have to find another way. Soon the evil figure was a mere speck receding into the blood red clouds.

As it disappeared, a few stray black feathers floated down and changed into black insects with pointed wings and poisonous stingers. Suddenly they encircled Iduna and attacked. She fought them off, but one crept into the folds of her gown and stung her to the heart. The swarm knew that one had succeeded and, satisfied, withdrew and flew away. The poison left behind was working to sap Iduna's strength. From that moment on, things began to go wrong.

Unaware of any danger to Iduna, Odin and Loki had departed on their journey. The travelers were a strange pair. Though half brothers, they could not have been more different. Odin was a mighty ruler careful to temper his great power with reason and compassion. Loki was a selfish mischief maker, capable of changing his shape as easily as his loyalties. He managed to stir up trouble whenever Odin was away. This time, hoping to thwart calamity, Odin had invited Loki to join him. Unfortunately, even a wise plan cannot prevent what is inevitable.

That evening, having traveled far, the two companions found a spot in the wilderness to rest for the night. Hungry, they set about building a fire to roast some meat for their supper. When the fire seemed quite hot, Odin covered the meat with the burning embers to hasten its cooking.

Presently, an ominous black bird, the very one that had plagued Iduna, soundlessly alighted in a tall tree above them. There, hidden in the shadows, the evil creature watched and waited, a vicious sneer twisting its human lips.

At last, Loki exclaimed, "I'm starving! It's been hours since that meat went in the fire. Surely it's cooked by now."

Odin answered, "It *has* been long enough. See if it's ready to eat."

But when they looked, the meat was raw. Disgusted, Loki sat back again to wait. More time passed, and again they checked the roast, but it was as before: The meat was too raw to eat.

Odin raised his eyes to Loki and frowned, saying, "However long we wait, this meat will not cook. No doubt there is some dark magic at work tonight."

His words brought a harsh laugh from the shadows. "Unless you share your meat with me," said the huge black bird, "I can assure you, you'll not eat tonight."

Odin knew at once that this was no real bird. He suspected that it was Thiassi, for the wicked giant often disguised himself as a bird of prey. But Odin could not be absolutely certain and, wishing to avoid trouble, agreed to the bird's demand. At once, the roast was ready to eat, whereupon Odin motioned to the bird to take its share. The creature flew down, took the very best portion, and left almost nothing for Odin and Loki.

Outraged, Loki seized a stick and struck the intruder. Instantly the bird took flight, carrying the stick in its talons with the startled Loki, his hands held fast, clinging to the other end. No matter how hard he tried, he could not let go.

The bird *was* Thiassi, and by his evil magic he held Loki bound. Thiassi flew low, dragging his helpless victim across the ground and through the trees. Bruised and bleeding, Loki pleaded for mercy. But Thiassi was the enemy of all the gods of Asgard. He had failed to capture Iduna, and thus he was delighted to carry off Loki, for he had a plan.

"I will set you free on one condition," said the giant as he flew dangerously close to a row of jagged cliffs.

"*Anything!* Anything you wish!" shouted Loki, his voice filled with terror at the sight of this new danger.

The giant laughed and said, "You are a coward, Loki, but you'll have your freedom, if you promise to deliver Iduna and her treasure of magic apples to me."

Loki agreed at once, without a thought to the consequences for Iduna or the gods, and visited the Everlasting Garden at the first opportunity.

He found Iduna alone, sitting in her apple orchard deep in thought. She did not see Loki until he sat down beside her.

"Iduna, guess where I have been," said Loki as he eyed her closely. "If you like, I'll tell you. But first, let me have one of your marvelous apples."

Iduna reached into the golden chest and handed him a shining apple.

But Loki tossed it from one hand to the other, without taking a bite. Giving her a sidelong glance, he frowned and said, "It's just as I suspected. Poor innocent girl, your apples are nothing compared to some I've seen recently."

Iduna was startled, but she tried to smile. "Surely you're mistaken," said Iduna. "Odin, who has traveled the world over, insists there are no apples to compare to these."

Loki laughed slyly, and the sound made the maiden uneasy. "Well, Odin is mistaken. He'll soon change his mind, I assure you."

His harsh words hurt her, and she stood up quickly. As she did, a sharp pain, like the point of a stinger, jabbed at her heart. She pressed her hand to the spot. "It would be better not to talk of this," she said, and started to walk away.

Loki knew the power of his words and hastened after her. "All right, don't listen to me. But you'll be sorry when your garden is forgotten and everyone is going to this new one for its apples. Alas, my dear, then it will be too late."

Iduna sighed. The poisoned stinger had done its work. She felt too weak to shake off these taunting words. As her strength ebbed away, Iduna's mind grew dark and confused.

Quickly, like a viper moving in for the kill, Loki continued. "Perhaps I should take you to this orchard — it's close by — so you can see for yourself if what I say is true. You mustn't take *my word* for it! Together we could gather all of the apples. Then I'll help you plant their seeds here in your own orchard. It'll be our secret. I swear I'll not tell anyone." With that, Loki came close to Iduna and took her hand in his, saying, "Oh, but you must come now, Iduna. We will go at once, before it's *too late*."

Iduna looked into Loki's eyes and asked, "Is it truly a short distance? I shouldn't leave my garden, but if you promise we'll return quickly…perhaps there is no harm."

"Quickly!" Loki exclaimed with a laugh. "We'll be back in no time at all. Don't tell me you can't leave this garden even for a few moments. I'm doing you a favor. Surely you won't refuse me?"

Resigned at last, Iduna reached for the chest and said, "All right, but we must hurry."

Still holding firmly to Iduna's hand, Loki began to run down the path toward the gate, heedless of whether she stumbled or struggled to catch her breath. She had no time to think as he pulled her along behind him. He didn't stop until they had reached the gate that shut the garden off from the rest of the world.

Iduna hesitated and tried to step back, but Loki tugged at her roughly, forcing her through the gate and out of the garden. In that final second she heard all the life in the garden cry out to her. *Iduna, don't abandon us! Oh, Iduna, please. Come back. Come back!*

But it was too late. The gate banged shut behind her. She stood with Loki on the other side of all she loved.

The sun was low on the horizon. An overgrown path ahead was deep in shadow. A chilly night wind blew through Iduna's hair, stung her cheeks, and made her shiver.

"We must be quick," Iduna whispered, "so I may come back soon."

Loki did not answer.

She looked at him, and his face was turned away from her, toward the dark sky above them. She followed his gaze and quaked with terror at what she saw. There looming over her was the wicked Thiassi, his wings spread wide. As he dropped lower and lower, his huge shadow fell over her like a cloak. Before she could find breath to cry out, the creature's black talons clasped her and she was lifted higher and higher into the sky.

Loki watched impassive till they vanished, then shrugged and said, "It's nothing to me if Thiassi wishes to make Iduna his captive. I will never be suspected."

Yet something disturbed him. Walking on, eyes fixed upon the ground, Loki tried to dismiss Iduna from his thoughts. He could not. Finally, he paused and asked himself, "What if Odin is right and Iduna's apples *are* the reason that we are all strong and youthful? Might *I* suffer and grow old without Iduna's magic apples? *Impossible!*" Yet he shuddered.

Loki heard a sound and looked up to see his daughter, Hela, mistress of the dead, drifting past him. She stopped a moment and glanced at Loki. The sight of her never failed to strike fear in her father. One side of her face was quite beautiful but deathly pale; the other, the white bones of death itself.

It was not long before the gods knew that Iduna had vanished, for almost at once the Everlasting Garden began to die. The flowers dropped their petals and withered, the leaves faded, and a harsh north wind howled through the grove and tore them from their branches. Dense gray clouds hung overhead, hiding all traces of the sun. The strong wind brought rain that soon changed to snow, smothering everything under a thick white mantle.

No matter where Loki turned, there were worried looks and anxious questions. "Where can Iduna have gone?" "How can it be that she has left her garden without a word to any of us?" *"Is there not one of us who knows more than he is saying?"*

Little by little, day by day, Iduna's absence took its toll on all of them. Lines of worry deepened into wrinkles. Their hair lost its luster and soon turned white. Sapped of their vigor, the once-immortal gods grew old.

It was then that Loki's daughter, Hela, appeared in Odin's palace, Valhalla. Odin commanded her to leave, but Hela laughed and answered, "I'll claim all of you soon enough. Without Iduna's apples to keep you young, none of you are safe from death. Your time grows short. I will leave, but only to make a place for you in my land of the *dead*!"

When she had gone, Bragi, Odin's son, spoke out. "We have ourselves to blame, if we cannot find Iduna. Many months have passed, and yet not one of us has gone to search for her. Tell me, are we all too feeble to risk our lives for her? Well, I am not."

Odin spoke up quickly. "Bragi is right. He and I will go at once to the three sisters of fortune. They'll tell us where to seek Iduna."

The sisters of fortune could tell the past, the present, and the future, but they answered in riddles that only the wise Odin could decipher. From them he and Bragi learned that it was Loki who had helped Thiassi steal Iduna. The sisters declared that only Loki could rescue her and undo the evil he had caused, and to reach the giant's ice palace he must fly there, using falcon wings.

Loki refused. The thought of facing the giant again was too terrible for such a coward. But the gods threatened him with death unless he agreed. Reluctantly, he let them fasten the mantle of falcon feathers upon his shoulders. At once, he was transformed into a bird and flew up into the sky toward Thiassi's castle.

As Loki drew closer and closer to his destination, the sky turned steel gray and the frosty air grew even colder. Finally, he saw the icy mountains that encircled Thiassi's domain; indeed, it was a land made totally of ice, dull and without luster, for the sun would not shine. Loki had never seen such a place. The entire castle was carved from the side of a huge ice mountain. Here the giant had imprisoned Iduna.

Fearing that the gods might one day discover her, Thiassi had shut Iduna in a chamber without light or fresh air, where she passed each day isolated and alone, seeing no one but Thiassi.

Once a day he visited to ask the same question. "When will you grant me what I ask, Iduna? I'll have the magic apples and *you* as my bride, mark my words! Sooner or later you must agree," roared the giant.

Iduna trembled but bravely resisted him and firmly said *no,* regardless of his threats. To give the magic apples to Thiassi, Iduna knew, would be disastrous, for in his hands their powers for good would turn to evil. He would have taken the apples by force, but they shrank to tiny seeds and slipped through his fingers whenever he reached into the golden chest. There in the corners they hid until Iduna placed her hand in the chest. Then the apples grew full and ripe again.

One morning, the giant went off across the ocean. Relieved to be free of him for a little while, Iduna went to the tiny crevice where, if she pressed her ear, she could hear the moaning of the sea far below. Oh, she thought, if only I could return to my own sweet garden.

Just then, she heard her name called. There outside the tiny opening was Loki, his falcon wings spread wide to steady himself against the gusty wind.

"Quickly," he shouted. "Get the golden chest."

"I have it," she answered, and Loki spoke a few words of magic. Instantly she was changed into a small gray bird, and the precious golden chest became a tiny locket hidden beneath her feathers.

Out the narrow window like an arrow came Iduna. The wind tore at her fragile wings, but she pressed on against the current.

"Follow me or we will both be lost forever," Loki shouted back at her. "This way lies the land of Asgard."

The thought of home and her beloved friends gave Iduna fresh strength, and her heart swelled with courage. "Thiassi shall not triumph!" she whispered, and with these determined words the little bird picked up speed.

But they had not gone far when they heard screams of rage behind them. It was the giant, who had returned to discover that Iduna had escaped. Turning himself back into a giant bird, he flew in pursuit.

For three long days and nights he chased them. Though they had had a head start, his speed exceeded theirs and he was narrowing the distance. Soon he would snatch up the tiny bird in his sharp talons.

Ever since Loki's departure, the gods had kept a vigil on Valhalla's high tower, watching for a sign. On the fourth night, the sharp-eyed Odin spotted a falcon and another, much smaller bird pursued by a massive black-winged creature.

Calculating the speed at which they each traveled, sadly he told the others, "They will not escape. Thiassi will seize Iduna before she can reach us."

Odin ordered fires set. By the time the flames were raging, the travelers were very close. Now all could see that the giant would seize Iduna before she could reach safety.

Suddenly, the falcon rose to escape the wall of flames. The small gray bird lifted herself to follow. But the giant black bird was too heavy to rise. The flames hungrily caught his sweeping wings, and he tumbled to his doom in the blaze.

With Iduna's last effort she passed over the clouds of smoke and came to rest at Odin's feet. He lifted her up with the touch of his hand, and Iduna was restored to her true form.

A glorious celebration soon followed. Songs were written that day of Iduna's triumph over Thiassi. In the halls of Valhalla the minstrels sang with such feeling that the very walls rang with their music. A great feast was spread across the polished banquet table. Iduna opened the golden chest and gave each of the gods a magic apple. As they ate, new vigor flowed into their veins and they were made strong and young once more.

At the close of the feasting, Iduna returned to the Everlasting Garden. The instant she reentered, the sun shone bright and warm again, and what had seemed dead in her absence was reborn. Springtime in all its beauty unfolded once more. The fair young trees grew tall and green and the flowers lifted their radiant heads at the sight of her. The wind's fragrant breezes blew softly through the grove in a song of praise for her, and the birds took up the melody, singing joyously of their beloved Iduna's return.